THE
SOUL
INFLUENCER

YOUTH WRITERS CHALLENGE SERIES, VOL 5

THE
SOUL
INFLUENCER

ESSENCE COTTON | TRISTAN COTTON | CATHERINE TAYLOR
JONATHAN TAYLOR | RALPH TAYLOR III | WILLIAM TAYLOR

THE SOUL INFLUENCER

Special discounts are available on bulk quantity purchases by book clubs, associations and special interest groups. For details email: sales@publishyourgift.com or call (888) 949-6228.
For information logon to: www.PublishYourGift.com

AUTHORS

Essence Cotton

Tristan Cotton

Catherine Taylor

Jonathan Taylor

Ralph Taylor III

William Taylor

Thank you to everyone who has supported the Youth Writers Challenge, Inc. and the Youth Writers Rock organizations.

Thank you to the instructors who helped with this project:
Patricia Johnson-Harris, Roger Harris,
Lazaria Foreman, Robin Stokes, Jackie JC Gardner,
Debrayta Salley, Jackie Anderson,
Nanette Buchannan, Pam Reaves, Rod Lopez,
Robyn F. Evans, and Joy Turner.

TABLE OF CONTENTS

PREFACE

It had been raining for several days and the lack of sunshine and blue skies was depressing. He needed sunlight to brighten his mood, but it seemed the weatherman had other plans.

Mr. Ambrose White was not a happy guy. He had loads of money from his tech businesses, which he had invested wisely over the years. He had a huge estate with a lot of property, including an Olympic-sized swimming pool, basketball courts, and horse stables. He had a chef, a housekeeper, a driver, and his multi-car garage housed eight vehicles—from sports cars to SUVs. They were always kept fresh and clean—immaculate like his seven-bedroom house. He had done massive renovations over the years, except for a part of the basement.

Even with all of this, he was still not happy or fulfilled. He was a very smart man but often overlooked because he just wasn't that attractive. He had ivory skin; he was on the short side and slim with thinning hair, thick glasses, and bushy eyebrows. His eyes were gray like the clouds, but no one ever noticed.

He craved the attention that he deserved! He wanted millions of social media followers, yet he only had a few hundred. He envied the popular social media influencers who barely did anything spectacular, yet they had followers all around the planet. They were loved, admired, imitated, and revered. They had unmatched power to change the world with just their appearance or words.

Just thinking about it got him angry. He wanted to be in their shoes, but as long as they were around, he didn't have a chance.

And it was then, at that moment—while sitting in his study, wearing a designer robe and slippers, and sipping on a vanilla Frappuccino while nibbling on a croissant—that he devised the most devious of plans.

Chapter 1

ORIGINS OF A MAD GENIUS

Catherine Taylor

The phrase "Ugly Duckling" is an understatement for him. When Ambrose was born, his head came out slightly misshapen with a lump at the top. His parents were a bit traumatized by it and decided not to have any other kids. Though this lump had no effect on his brain and other vital organs, he would forever look like something was wrong with him. But nothing was wrong with him; in fact, his brain worked a lot faster than others.

By the time Ambrose was in kindergarten, he could read and write fluently, which sucked for him when it came time for other students to read to the class. The pace at which other students were reading was agonizingly slow.

Two weeks into the school year, a student named Susan paused before the word "the." It took her thirteen full seconds before she finally attempted to read it, and five-year-old Ambrose was fed up with how long she was taking.

He shouted, "It's … just … three … letters!"

He immediately put his hands over his mouth after his outburst, and everyone's eyes instantly flew to him. This was the first time the class had heard him speak in that manner because Ambrose was usually quietly working or playing by himself. Susan looked at him first with surprise, then indignation, and finally with anger.

"That's why nobody likes you, Hump Head!" Susan shot back.

The class howled with laughter at the insult. Ambrose never spoke up in class after that, embittered by everyone's reaction. His demeanor toward his classmates became darker, always clouded by anger for those who made fun of him. But after a while, his ostracism made him feel lonelier than anything, and he regretted not speaking to anyone.

No one wanted him as a friend now.

When Ambrose was a senior in high school, he was valedictorian of his class, but he never gave a speech, never publicly received an award, never joined a club, and he *never* had a friend. Not for lack of trying. The man desired friends, but no one *wanted him*.

His parents never even took a photo of him—no baby pictures, no sports, no dances. There was no permanent documentation of him except what was required by the government.

But that was all about to change.

Ambrose wasn't ignorant. He could see that those deemed "popular and important" didn't like him because they thought they were better than him or that he was unworthy of them. Other students, despite being caught off guard by his head, didn't hold any distaste for Ambrose. They were just afraid of being ostracized by the so-called "cool kids" for associating with him.

His thoughts ran rampant: *Stupid popular people! If it weren't for their monopoly on what was socially acceptable, I'd have friends right now.* Having convinced himself that his situation wasn't at all the consequence of secluding himself for so long before reaching out, he redirected his thoughts to his plan for people to like him. *I may look like a freak, but no one can deny that I'm a genius. When I show how smart I am in the upcoming school science fair, people will have to approve of me then. Why wouldn't they?*

For Ambrose, science, technology, and math came easy. His father set up a lab for him in their basement where he was able to tinker with circuits, gears, and small machines. For example, one day he repaired his family's old, oversized TV with a wire kit his father got him. It was the brightest he'd ever seen his father smile.

Thoroughly convinced his plan would work, he brought his invention to the science fair. The device was going to use the base idea of hypnosis to remove problems with employees that made bad decisions for selfish reasons, like disloyalty, corporate espionage, or theft from the company. This device would remove any possibility of an employee stealing, spying, or destroying property on purpose. He knew that neural stimulators could be used to either relax the brain or keep it in its current state, normally for up to eight hours.

Hypnosis users use repetition of words or mental images to help a person focus, then offer possibilities for new thoughts, feelings, or perspectives chosen as the goals of the treatment. His device was an earpiece with a tiny satellite inside. It first relaxes the brain, then suggests the full commitment and loyalty to the individual's job, and finally keeps the brain in that state for as long as the earpiece is on (which isn't forever).

Entering the auditorium was a nerve-wracking experience, as Ambrose had made a point not to participate in extracurricular activities, focusing all his energy on his invention. However, despite not being a part of a club, Ambrose was a part of a small select group of students whose experiments were a bit more sophisticated. While others were growing plants, firing rockets, and using construction paper for their trifolds, this special group went one at a time on stage to present their findings to the school as a part of the "Gifted and Talented" group. As he made his way to the stage, he felt everyone eyeing the lump on his head, and it didn't help that he didn't have a lot of hair. The room was also noisy; not many people cared to hear his presentation. Ambrose summoned up his pride and walked to the center of the stage with his invention.

He had rehearsed at home with his parents, who thought it was incredible, but that's what parents always say. He cleared his throat and grabbed the microphone.

"Ladies and gentlemen, esteemed faculty and guests, I have an invention for you today that will eliminate all employee infidelity without causing any harm."

Everyone quieted at his intro. An almost visible "Huh?" hung in midair. Ambrose continued.

"My device is a comfortable earpiece with a tiny satellite dish inside that plays a soft frequency that begins a small form of hypnosis," the young genius explained as he held up the device.

"First, the brain is relaxed and its guards are lowered, leaving the mind open to suggestion. Next, the idea of commitment is placed into the subconscious. Finally, without even thinking about it, the employee will behave exactly as they're supposed to, without any impediments on their personality or feelings."

Ambrose paused, waiting for a reaction. He couldn't see the crowd over the glare of the lights pointing at him from the ceiling to light the stage, and he hoped they couldn't see the sweat on his brow starting to form.

There was complete silence. Then after a couple of seconds, someone chuckled, then two people, then the whole room laughed at the ridiculousness of the idea.

"Oh please, no way!" some shouted.

"Woah, woah, woah! Hold on, your idea is to hypnotize people to do whatever their employers want them to!? You're crazy!" shouted another.

Ambrose was stunned. How could they not see the implications of this technology? The infinite possibilities and benefits of eliminating the ability to choose wrong?

He pleaded, "But think about the possibilities! We could get rid of crime, eliminate selfishness, make *everyone* acceptable to *society!*"

This had to work, they had to see that this could work. No one would choose to do the wrong thing again because they'd have *no choice*. He could fix all the problems in the world that stemmed from stupid decisions.

Ambrose was thinking, *People wanting to fit in with the crowd for their own benefit instead of choosing to care is why I am always rejected, because society has decided that ugly equates to worthlessness. My invention is perfect; it's not me, it's these people.*

He was laughed at and booed off the stage, while the teachers tried to calm everyone down.

Their reaction only hardened his heart.

Before he went home, his science teacher tried to praise him for his work (albeit hesitantly, as mind control wasn't something he wanted Ambrose to aspire to). But Ambrose could not receive the compliments.

When he got home, Jeanette, his mother, tried to console him after he explained what happened.

"Honey," his mother said, holding his face in her hands, "you can't let them get to you. There will always be people like that in the world. We can't choose our neighbors, we just have to love them," she said sweetly.

"But they don't have to be like that! I can fix them!" he argued.

"Only one can fix the human heart. Whether or not people want their heart fixed is entirely up to them."

But why give them the choice? the eighteen-year-old thought.

Easily discerning his train of thought, Ambrose's mother gently said, "Every human has free will—the ability to choose for his or herself what to do and how to think. It is the way we use our free will that shows who we are and what we care about, be it others or only ourselves. Sadly, we as human beings often use our free will selfishly, even at the expense of others, and it hurts us as well."

Exactly! Ambrose thought. *People always choose to be selfish!*

His mother continued, "But that doesn't mean that the solution is to take away free will. That would render humanity a never-ending machine void of anything unique or meaningful," Jeanette finished sternly.

What else can I do to make people do the right thing? Free will is the only thing standing between us and a perfect world. And if the world won't make that choice, I'll make it for them.

Resigning himself to the idea that no one would ever accept him willingly, the eighteen-year-old came to a decision that he would not share with his dear mother. He would no longer challenge her thoughts, but instead let her have the last word.

But on the inside, he thought, *Fine, if I can't get the people to accept me for my genius, then they'll accept me because they have no choice.*

Chapter 2

COLLEGE TALES: AMBROSE FINDS A HOME

Catherine Taylor and William Taylor

Although Ambrose loved his parents, he couldn't stand living in a community that only ever saw the lump on his head and looked at him as the butt of all jokes. But accepted or not, Ambrose was a genius. The bright young man easily got into Virginia Tech based on merit. The students were surprised by his arrival in the class, and even more surprised to figure out that he really belonged there.

Going to Virginia Tech was a pleasurable experience. This illustrious college was the first institution to really challenge and educate Ambrose. Plus, he was finally with his intellectual peer group, where his genius was *actually acknowledged* and appreciated. One classmate in particular, Travis, his lab partner, seemed unperturbed by Ambrose's head lump and talked to him normally. Ambrose appreciated him and was glad to call Travis his friend.

While working on a circuit board together, the older classmate said to Ambrose, impressed, "I'm sorry that it's taken this long for you to get here. I bet with your grades you could have graduated way early, so why did you choose to wait?"

The younger scholar's face darkened a bit. "My condition made it so no one wanted to be my friend, but I stayed because I thought that if I showed everyone a cool invention, they'd like it and accept me based on merit rather than who's popular."

Travis nodded, "Ah," he said, "and after finally making your mark, you came here to refine your inventing skills," Travis guessed.

"No, after getting laughed off the stage, I came here to escape the constant judgment and rejection from the place I grew up in, and to figure out how I can use my technological genius to change the way people think so they'll want to stop behaving stupidly."

Ambrose was surprised at how open he was with Travis, probably because he'd never been told he was wanted by someone other than his parents.

"Well, if you want to change the way people behave, you should become an influencer," Travis joked.

Ambrose raised an eyebrow at that. Influencers, Ambrose thought, were just people who recorded themselves and put their lives on display for others' viewing pleasure.

In response to the question in Ambrose's eyes, Travis said, "Yeah, they make a living off of getting people to like them and then telling them what's cool and what's not. A lot of people's decisions and behaviors are heavily affected by influencers, even how they think and feel about things, which is why businesses call them to promote their products." He paused briefly to take a breath, then continued schooling Ambrose. "Influencers encourage people to buy products and that's how they make money."

Ambrose soaked in all of Travis' insights.

So, I can't take away choice militaristically with force, but with influence, I can change people's feelings and decisions without them even noticing that they're being controlled by my influence! If I had this kind of power paired with my technology, there's no one I couldn't control!

A small, sly grin came across Ambrose's face as the wheels turned within his mind about how to take this newfound information and turn it into gold! Travis noticed that his friend's demeanor changed. But before he could ask him what was going on, Ambrose escaped to the lab.

Using the tech labs at his college, the reinvigorated inventor developed sound technology, including speakers, headphones, earbuds, and even satellite dishes. After graduating, he patented the devices and began to sell them as a new brand. The superior sound quality of these new speakers and earbuds made them sell quickly, and before the young inventor turned twenty-nine, he owned a thriving, multimillion-dollar business.

In this day and age, it is possible to never leave your house and still get any necessity. Everything from ordering food and clothes to having doctor's visits can be done online. Ambrose used this to his advantage in running his company. Since his head lump disturbed clients, he did business calls virtually. His company, Auditory Perception, was recognized only by the brand name. The master inventor's business had spread across America, a vast network of sound and signal working together.

Instead of trying to create his own sphere of influence, he'd just take over the ones that were already there. He'd steal their creative *souls* and use them for his good. He had two types of earpieces. One for the regular consumer and ones that were equipped with hypnosis technology. He wanted to be very strategic about who had the hypnosis version, although with a pair of his earpieces in almost every home in America, he could have used his hypnosis technology on anyone who had theirs on.

But there was a flaw in Ambrose's scheme—the moment someone's earpiece was removed or lost power, they were jarred out of hypnosis and he lost control of them. This put a damper on his plan to control the most influential influencers to persuade people to want, well, whatever he wanted them to. If one of the influencers caught on because their earpiece died mid-promotion, millions of people at once would know that something was up. Ambrose needed to make the signal permanent. Not that they'd be under his control forever, they'd just be forever "standing by" so to speak. But to do that, he'd need to get up close and personal with these influencers for a while.

Kidnapping seemed like the only way Ambrose could ever work on influencers for a long period of time. He paused at the realization that if he wanted this to work, he'd have to resort to criminal activity and take people against their will.

Hmmmm, Ambrose contemplated. *Is it worth it to kidnap these people?*

He wondered for a brief moment as he stared at the walls with dozens of screens on them, all showing different influencers—singers, gymnasts, gamers, fitness coaches, and even preachers.

Yes, he decided, *I should be in control. People can't be trusted to make good decisions on their own. As far as I'm concerned, they don't make their own decisions anyway. All of them are so consumed with social media and material things, they don't see the impact of the weight they put on the words and actions of people they've never even met. If my plan works and they allow their free will to be taken away, it's their fault.*

But where would he put them? Ambrose stood still and contemplated this. Then, a flickering light from his basement caught his attention.

Well, that answers that question! he thought.

The unfinished area of his basement was the perfect place to house his temporary guests. Ambrose hired a contractor to begin construction. The basement area would be several bunk beds in a large space, not luxurious, but comfortable with two small bathrooms. He had to wait a year for most of his basement to be done, except for one small section, but he knew he couldn't rush this. When the construction was complete, he installed gadgets, security cameras and high-tech locks to which only he had the key.

With the rooms ready at last, Ambrose was finally able to start kidnapping influencers, but he could not do it alone. He needed someone physically fit but also easy to control. Strangely enough, during one of his rare adventures in public, he spotted the perfect candidate.

The reclusive businessman was out of his house in order to get the necessary sunlight on his skin. He wore a hat and a hood to make doubly sure that no one saw his head lump.

On that particular day, he was headed to the store, and a masked man bumped into him and picked his pocket.

Ambrose was caught completely off guard and quickly shouted, "HEY! Stop! Thief!" Not his most eloquent work. He yelled louder, "He has my wallet!"

A security guard by the door of the store heard the shout and raced to catch the mugger. The frustrated thirty-one-year-old watched as the guard chased the thief down the street. After about ten yards, the robber tripped and fell hard on the pavement, allowing the guard to cuff him then call the police.

Ambrose watched with relief and gratitude as the security guard came to return his wallet. He noticed a few things. The guard's uniform was messy, his eyes had bags under them, and though he was in excellent physical condition, he heaved very big breaths as though he'd run a mile.

"Here's your wallet, Sir," the tired man gasped between breaths.

"Thank you, and I'm so sorry for the trouble. Allow me to treat you to lunch sometime soon," Ambrose offered. What's your name?"

"Bastian Brown, Sir. And yes, please, lunch sounds great," Bastian eagerly accepted.

They exchanged contact information and met up for lunch later that week at the Wild Buffalo Bar and Grill. Bastian looked no better rested than before, if not less so. Ambrose took his hat off and laid his condition bare. Bastian looked taken aback, maybe weirded out, but not disgusted, which Ambrose was grateful for.

"Forgive me but, do you sleep?" Ambrose asked.

"Yeah, some, but I have bills to pay and there aren't enough hours in the day to pay 'em all," the younger man replied, sounding defeated.

"You seem strong and intelligent. Who put you in debt?" Ambrose asked candidly.

"No one. Look, my sister is sick. The doctors are treating her, but it costs twice what I earn doing security work, and it's hard to keep up, even when I take extra jobs. But if I don't, they'll stop the treatment and she'll …" The worn-out guard trailed off despondently with a sheen in his eyes.

Ambrose couldn't believe his luck! This was exactly the type of assistant he was looking for.

"What if I could help you with that?" Ambrose offered.

"How?" Bastian asked eagerly, sitting forward in his chair.

"How good are you at being a security guard?" Ambrose asked, having the perfect plan for Bastian.

"I'm tired but you saw that I can handle myself," Bastian reassured him.

"Do you know who I am?"

Bastian shook his head no, an embarrassed apology written on his face.

"I run Auditory Perception, or AP if you will. In fact, I'm the founder. I can give you a job that will provide for you and your sister. It comes with benefits and bonuses, so long as you deliver." Ambrose posed like the businessman he was.

The word "deliver" caused Bastian to pause. The offer was starting to sound shady. Wariness took over Bastian's demeanor, and he stiffened in his seat.

"Define *deliver*," Bastian commanded, as an officer would a criminal.

"It's simple. I want you to be my private security detail. I will provide you with a house, medical coverage for both you and your sister, and a bonus. If you must know everything, I plan on using some media influencers to promote my company, and I need your help to transport them. I need someone strong enough to deal with the less ... *compliant* ones."

Oops, Ambrose thought, *that wasn't subtle at all.*

Bastian instantly knew this was wrong. Ambrose was clever enough to phrase his offer in such a way that it could be taken a few different ways, but Bastian knew he shouldn't go through with it, even if that meant working harder to pay for his sister's treatment.

"I'm sorry, Sir. Your offer is a very generous one, but I can't accept. That's my final decision," Bastian said with his jaw set while looking straight at Ambrose.

"That's a shame, but I respect your decision," Ambrose said.

But he knew he couldn't let Bastian get away. The food arrived and they ate in silence.

As he paid the bill, Ambrose said, "Here, take this on the house as a parting gift." Ambrose passed him a box that held one of his brand's earpieces. "The sound quality on these is far superior to walkie talkies, and I see you still have that wired headphone to talk to people on your cell phone. I promise, these are ten times better. And if you change your mind about the job, give me a call."

He handed Bastian a business card.

Bastian wrinkled his brow, confused yet intrigued.

Who gets a gift for turning down a job? Bastian thought as he put the earpiece in his ear and switched it on, just as Ambrose wanted him to.

As soon as the light on it turned green, the security guard relaxed, then focused, cueing Ambrose that the earpiece worked.

Under the table, Ambrose manipulated a neurotransmitter. Bastian's eyes glossed over. He had him! Ambrose smiled a toothy grin.

"Well, Bastian, looks like you got a new job."

Chapter 3

BASTIAN BROWN: THE PERFECT TARGET!

Catherine Taylor and William Taylor

Bastian Brown is a very strong and caring guy. He loves his twin sister, Hope, more than anything because she is the only family he has. They're twins. At the age of five, their single mother abandoned them, and they were placed in foster care. He was always very protective of his sister, and they were blessed that they were never separated. But they also never had a family agree to adopt them, so they bounced from home to home. At the last placement, they managed to stay for four years until they aged out of the system at age eighteen.

It was hard being tossed out into the world with no real home to go back to. Even with those odds against them, they had their foster parents who were supportive but strict. They really wanted him and his sister to go to college, but Bastian didn't like school that much. Instead, he took low-paying jobs—in retail, at the factory, and at the gas station—just to support them. The military was an option, but he just could not leave Hope. She was really smart, got into college on a four-year scholarship, and followed her dreams to be a preschool teacher.

They lived together in a modest studio apartment near Washington, D.C. The space was small, but it accommodated twin beds, a kitchen, a small den, and a bathroom.

Once Hope graduated, she quickly got a job and promised to move them out of their cramped apartment. She even bought them a used car. Things were looking up, but then tragedy struck.

Just two years after graduating from college, Hope started having a lot of headaches and it affected her job as a teacher. Sadly, she was diagnosed with a brain tumor and had to stop working. Bastian was working extra hours at the parcel store, but it was still hard to pay for Hope's hospital stay, her medicine, and their apartment. The siblings had no one they could ask for money. She was eventually let go from her job and that left Bastian as the sole provider.

These thoughts and more weighed heavily on his mind as he pulled into his job's parking lot. Every day was a struggle for real. He and Hope applied for every social service program available, and they got some help, but it wasn't enough. Bastian needed money and he needed it fast.

He went into the storefront of Parcels for Less and greeted his boss who didn't have any kind of decorum; he would just get to the point without so much as a "good morning."

"Bastain, your orders are to mail this package to Phil in London, this package to Sally in Switzerland, and this package to Susan in Sweden."

Bastian looked at the packages covered in brown paper with the handwritten addresses.

"But, Sir, I can't do that!"

"Why not? You did it last week ... or did you?"

Bastian felt his face get hot. The fact was he couldn't remember how to use the machine last week and his co-worker, Jasmine, did all of the work. Clearly his boss, Ethan, found out. Anxiety began to fill his heart. He simply could not lose his job.

Ethan stood eye to eye with Bastian. Both of them were about 5'9" but Bastian was thin, and Ethan was portly with tousled hair and over-sized bifocals. He was upset but he was also empathetic.

"Look, Bastian, you've made six mistakes this week, including shipping some other packages to the wrong destination, and it's only Wednesday!"

"I understand, Sir. I'm sorry, Sir. It won't happen again, I promise," Bastian said with his head hung low.

"Look," Ethan replied, "I know you're in a rough spot right now because of your sister. And I know that if you're distracted it's because you love her and you're worried for her. I respect that. So instead of letting you go, I'm transferring you to a different job."

Bastian furrowed his brow. "A different job, Sir? But where?"

Ethan said, "Well, this store needs some security, so you'll be our security guard. You're a strong guy, and the training won't be too hard for you," his boss concluded, sounding more sympathetic than angry.

Bastian's face lit up so brightly he could guide a ship at night.

"Thank you so much, Mr. Ethan! I won't let you down. I know I can do this job," Bastian shouted with joy at his boss.

"I know you can. But remember, I can only give so many chances. Use this one wisely. And if you can find a better job, go for it. I know you and your sister need all the help you can get," his boss stated.

Bastian was ecstatic as he left the office with a new security job.

If there was one thing to know about Bastian, it was not to mess with his twin sister. Bastian recalled a time in third grade when the class idiot thought it'd be funny if he replaced the gummy worms in her lunchbox with real worms. Hope screamed at the sight of them wiggling around in her bag. Everyone's eyes flew toward the terrified sound, but Bastian *moved*. He flew over to the table where his sister sat and calmed her down with a hug. He sat with her and shared his lunch.

The idiot who did it, however, had the bright idea of bragging to everyone about his prank once the teachers were out of earshot and cleaning up the mess. The second his boasting reached Bastian's ears, he was on the ground. None of the teachers saw Bastian hit him and when they asked what happened, several eyes flickered over to Bastian then quickly looked away. No one was dumb enough to try something like that again.

Bastian chuckled as he recalled punching that guy. The memory was over two decades old and times seemed so much simpler back then. Now Hope was in real danger and he couldn't punch it away. With that grim thought, Bastian pulled into the hospital parking lot, bracing himself for the sight he'd be met with inside. He checked in and walked the familiar path to the room where his sister was receiving her weekly cancer treatments.

"Hey, bro! What are you doing here? Shouldn't you be at the postal job?" Hope asked, her joy just barely dulled by her confusion.

"Uhhhh, so about that …" Bastian started hesitantly before Hope cut him off.

"You got transferred to a security job because you mailed packages to entirely wrong continents, didn't you?" Hope interjected.

"Wha-! How did you guess that!?" Bastian sputtered while thinking, *Do I really suck that much?!*

"Ethan called me and let me know how distracted you've been lately, and that he was giving you this job as a last chance because he was good friends with our foster parents," Hope explained a bit more soberly.

"Oh, well. Don't worry. I won't screw up this job. You're going to be fine," Bastian reassured her.

"Bastian, I love you, but my brain tumor isn't getting any smaller. I don't want you to spend all of your time, energy, and money on me. Live your life, Bastian! Have a wife and kids! I know you want to be a father," Hope said with love in her voice, reminding Bastian why he hadn't let himself think about his life.

"Don't be ridiculous. How could I think about myself at a time like this? The only thing that matters is your health, not mine, and not anyone else's."

That last remark was a dark one and Bastian grimaced at his own words. Bastian's new job of being a security officer mirrored his strong desire to protect his sister and doing what he could to help her heal. He could do that by keeping up with her medical bills and excelling at his job.

"Bastian, you can't think like that! You have to remember that you and everyone else matter just as much as I do! If you disregard the value of others, you'll be ok with hurting them, and that can't happen."

Hope was disconcerted by her brother's comment. She saw how he wasn't dealing with her worsening condition well, and worse yet, he was putting it all on himself.

Bastian went quiet at his sister's response but quickly recovered and moved the conversation to lighter, happier topics. Hope was still concerned, but not wanting to fight, she let the topic drop. They talked about happy memories from their elementary and high school years, purposefully avoiding talking about middle school, as that was an embarrassing three years for both of them. The evening ended on a high note, but Bastian didn't sleep soundly, fearing that even though he got a last chance, he wouldn't make enough to keep paying for his sister's treatment. She would be back home the next day, where she would be weak and nauseous.

Over the next few weeks, he went through security guard training. Days after his training was complete, Bastian was standing there where he'd been posted, keeping a subtle but watchful eye on passersby and customers. One man in particular—a lean, young white fellow—seemed strangely concerned about keeping his hat on tight, fiddling with it over and over. He was almost like a stereotypical TV criminal who felt the need to pull the collar of their shirt up all the time. Bastian pulled his gaze away after a few seconds, though, refusing to get distracted again. And just as his thoughts began to drift back to his sister …

"HEY! Stop! Thief!" The man was pointing at the assailant. "He has my wallet!" The lean man yelled.

Bastian chased the thief down the street. The mugger didn't get far before he tripped and fell hard on the ground, a situation Bastian would otherwise find comical. He cuffed him and called the police to officially arrest him.

The slender man looked relieved and grateful as Bastian handed him his wallet. Bastian could see the man taking note of his appearance, which made him want to shy away since he knew he didn't look very professional. He heaved multiple breaths even though he hadn't run much, but he felt accomplished.

"Here's your wallet, Sir," Bastian said while trying to catch his breath.

"Thank you, and I'm so sorry for the trouble. Allow me to treat you to lunch sometime soon."

Chapter 4

JENNIFER GOMEZ: PRIVATE EYE

Ralph Taylor III and Tristan Cotton

It was Friday morning. Jennifer awoke to the sound of her alarm clock ringing. She sleepily lifted her arms, found her phone, and swiped to snooze but instead turned off the alarm all together. After going back to sleep for what felt like a few minutes, she lifted her heavy eyes, looked at the clock, and saw that it was 6:30! She'd overslept! She rushed to the bathroom, did her shoulder-length hair enough so that she didn't still have bed head, brushed her teeth, put on her favorite navy-blue sweatshirt and ripped jeans, got her backpack, and checked the mirror one last time.

She was satisfied with her rushed look, noting she looked just like her dad—average height with cocoa-colored skin, brown eyes, and high cheekbones. Her mother was more fair-skinned, a blend of many flavors, most notably Italian and Spanish. Her brother resembled her mother.

After a last check of her appearance, she hurried to her bus stop on Wellington Road to find the bus was about to leave.

"Wait, wait for me!!!" She waved and yelled frantically for it to stop, running hard to try and catch it.

Unfortunately, the bus driver didn't hear her yelling and she missed the bus. She angrily yelled out, "Arghhhh!!"

Frustrated and annoyed, she now had to think of a new way to get to school on time. She was always running late, and her parents left early for their jobs, so they weren't home. Not only that, she dare not call and tell them once again she missed the bus. And her brother was always working, so he couldn't help either. There were times he let her use his car but not often.

Jennifer checked to see if she had money for an Uber, but no such luck. That meant she had to walk! She hung her head at the thought of walking the mile and a half to school, but she had no choice other than to get going, knowing she would be late to her first period class and maybe even second period. She began her trek, and after a couple of blocks, she was about to pop in her earbuds for some musical motivation.

At that moment, a person that she knew from school was driving by with his parents. His name was Jason, and he was known as one of the best people when it came to technology and construction. Jennifer waved to try to get him to stop, but he just kept rolling on. She got *really* mad at him. And as she was furiously eyeing him driving away, a car drove up next to her.

"Jennifer, right?" the guy asked after rolling down his window.

Jennifer looked over to see the familiar face of Marvin Moore. They didn't talk a whole lot, but they saw each other often on the way to school and in the hallways.

Jennifer said, "Hey, Marvin, right?"

"You need a ride? I can take you to school," he offered graciously.

Jennifer hesitated a bit, not really one to jump into anybody's car, but she felt safe enough to accept his offer. It was awkward for the first part of the ride, then Marvin decided to speak up.

"So, how was your week?" he asked nervously.

"It's been ok. I've been swamped in some work."

"Really?" he said, rather surprised. "I hear that you usually have no problem with schoolwork."

Marvin knew that because Jennifer was constantly at the top of the honor roll at school.

"It's not schoolwork. It's this little mystery I've been working on," Jennifer said, shyly.

"What kind of mystery?" Marvin asked curiously.

She excitedly replied, "It's on the influencers that have been going missing!"

The disappearance of popular influencers was something that kept Jennifer up late at night. She hoped to be a private investigator or something in the criminal justice field once she got out of high school. She loved solving problems, and she had been working on some new connections to this mystery and was trying to see where they fit in her notes.

About eight months ago, she noticed that a singer, Taylana Swiffy, had vanished from social media. She didn't post a goodbye video, and her people didn't post anything that said she was leaving for vacation, business, or a break. She just disappeared. After that, Jennifer started to notice how a few other influencers of all kinds, every couple of weeks or so, went missing.

When she looked online to see what other people were posting about it, everyone looked at it like the influencers were just leaving at the peak of their success and enjoying life. Jennifer was always annoyed with that answer and started doing some research of her own. She looked at the plans the influencers had and the things they said.

She researched their income, their content, *anything* she could think of or find. She was quick with work at school, so homework wasn't that much of an obstacle in her research time.

"Hmmm," Marvin responded, "I saw that on the news a while ago but didn't think about it too much. You think something suspicious is going on?"

"Well, we can talk about it later, at lunch perhaps?" Jennifer asked with a raised eyebrow.

"Yeah, that seems good."

They then arrived at school and departed to their classes.

Chapter 5

JASON TYLER JONES: THE SKEPTIC

Jonathan Taylor

It was an average life—a house in the Blue Ridge Mountains, two parents, three children, school, friends, the whole shebang. Jason was the middle child and had a special relationship with his older sister, Janet. She took Jason and his younger sister, Julia, to a special spot in the mountains with a beautiful sunset and a perfect view of the entire city.

Jason's mother was a teacher and his father was a woodcarver. He grew up wanting to create something and practiced every day with things he had in his home, from wood to building blocks, but mostly with Lego's. He was very mechanically and technologically intelligent and knew how a lot of things worked so he was able to fix and make several things, like a remote-controlled car with a claw to pick stuff up.

He was on the tall side, 5'11", with black, mildly spiked hair. His light skin was always covered by short-sleeve shirts and sweatpants. He was lean like a track runner, despite not really participating in physical activities.

Blue Ridge Park was a calm and quiet place, so Jason and his family were happy there. But his parents' jobs weren't very high paying, so their financial situation was rapidly deteriorating.

Everything changed when Jason turned fifteen. A very rich man came to their home. Apparently, the man worked with several schools to find the best and brightest talent they had to offer in the area of technology. He wanted to get to them before the larger corporations, like Google or Apple, did. Noone in Jason's family had ever heard of the wealthy man, but *he had the bills to get Jason's skills.* He called himself Mr. Emevas. He commended Jason for his technological prowess and gave Jason an IQ test. Jason, according to the test, had an IQ of 153.

The man offered Jason a high-paying job to be a technology developer, but on the condition that he and his family had to leave the mountainous region. The man wanted to buy their land to build a new headquarters, where Jason would ultimately work. He offered Jason's family $5 million to settle in Arlington, Virginia.

Jason, being fifteen, was underage and couldn't work at the corporation like a full-time employee. Until he turned eighteen, he would take online orientation classes for the job on Wednesdays to learn what he'd be doing there. On the other days, however, he'd be attending Arlington Community High School.

His family graciously accepted the offer and made the move to Arlington, but Jason had to leave everything behind—his friends, his school, and his special place.

Jason settled in relatively well, but he didn't really care for politics or things that happened in the world and hated listening to all the conspiracy theories going around the school. Someone was always making stuff up about things happening in the world that couldn't even be verified.

Jason breezed through his classes, but often after school, he went straight home to work on his own Lego projects or log on to get training for his job that he would start once he graduated.

One particular school day, little did Jason know, the band Owl City was touring through Virginia. He really liked the band, and if he had known they were in town, he would have tried to get tickets. He had skipped lunch to study with his history teacher, so on his way home, he decided to stop by a Taco Bell. Standing in line right in front of him was the lead singer of the band, Adam Young. Jason couldn't believe it. He looked around for the other band members, but Adam appeared to be alone. Jason wouldn't have even recognized Adam with his fedora and dark shades on, but he was known for the dragon tattoo on his neck. Adam was all over social media with millions of followers. He was probably staying at the Regency Hotel, where all of the mega stars stayed, just three blocks away.

Jason was nervous but he had to find out if this was indeed Adam. The man in line was shorter than Jason had imagined.

It was totally out of character for Jason, but he whispered under his breath, "Adam. Are you *thee* Adam Young?"

Adam turned around quickly and put his fingers to his lips.

"Shhh … yeah, it's me. I had to break away from the group and that lame hotel food. Please keep it to yourself, okay?"

Jason smiled, nodding, "Yeah, your secret is safe with me. Love your music."

He wished he had the nerve to ask for concert tickets, but he didn't.

Adam got his food and quickly left. Jason got his food too, and as he was leaving, he heard loud talking. When he turned the corner, he saw Adam talking to a person who looked like one of Owl City's bodyguards. It seemed like the person wanted him to accept something, but Adam kept giving it back. Then, the strange man grabbed Adam aggressively while shoving something into his ear. Suddenly, Adam wasn't aggressive anymore. He was almost robot-like as he got into the black vehicle. The bodyguard shook his fists in the air, smiling, like he was celebrating.

Jason knew something was wrong. He watched the truck drive in the opposite direction of the hotel. He felt helpless because he couldn't stop it and he surely didn't want to be kidnapped next, so he ran away.

Normally, Jason's parents picked him up, but this time he hopped on a shuttle bus that went close to his house. It was a quick ride. Once home, he felt rattled and had to talk to someone, but he didn't want to worry his parents. Who knows, maybe it was a publicity stunt.

Hoping for help, he logged onto his computer for his intern assignment and decided to share with his boss. He jumped right into the conversation.

"Mr. E., you won't believe what I just saw! There was a black truck, and Owl City, and what I believe was a kidnapping and ..." Jason's nerves had him rambling.

"Whoa, whoa, whoa!" Mr. E. responded. "Slow down! Kidnapping? Are you sure you've been getting enough sleep?"

"Yes, Sir, I'm sure of what I saw!"

"You might have eaten some bad food, or maybe ..."

"Sir, I know what I saw," Jason interjected. "I didn't hallucinate or dream it. I actually saw Adam Young from Owl City get kidnapped ... or something!"

"Ok, Jason. You didn't go to the police first, so I see you're not thinking straight. I guess that's a good thing though."

"What?" Jason responded, somewhat shocked by Mr. E's response.

"I'm gonna be straight with you. But first, let me ask you a question. Do you have any proof?"

Jason shook his head, "No, I don't."

How stupid of me, he thought, *to not have recorded the incident.*

"Look, it's not a good idea to contact the police or the media about this. You will look like a fool," Mr. E. said. "And if you tell anyone about this and bring negative attention to my company, you will lose this opportunity and all the money we gave your family. So, keep quiet. It's for your own good. You understand what I'm saying?"

Jason's heart sank. He knew what he saw, but he had no choice but to take his boss's advice to protect his family.

"Yes, Sir, I understand," Jason responded while averting his eyes and hanging his head in defeat.

"Good! Now that we've gotten that out of the way, I have a random question for you. It seems like you like music. You were into this band Owl City, huh?"

Jason sighed, not in the mood for small talk. He looked up at his boss, "Yeah, sure."

"What do you think about this singer, this girl, um, Ashanley Blued or something like that."

Jason thought for a moment, then said, "Do you mean A'Shantie Bleu? She's really good and getting loads of attention."

Mr. E. smiled. "Yes, exactly! That's all I needed to know. Now have a good night."

The call ended abruptly, leaving Jason a bit confused.

He was dismayed that Mr. E. had said to not tell the authorities about the incident or he could lose all the money his family needed and the job opportunity.

Jason didn't know what to do, so he decided to try to proceed with life as normally as he could. He didn't sleep very well that night. The next day, while his father was driving him to school, they passed Jennifer Gomez, one of the conspiracy theorists at his school. It seemed like she had missed her bus, but Jason had had enough of people talking about politics and stuff like that.

But seeing her made Jason think about all of the influencers' disappearances he'd seen on the news. And then there was a segment about Adam abandoning the band, which made Jason feel even worse! He started to consider if the theories might be true. But first, he needed to get through the day.

Chapter 6

MARVINMOORE:FITFORADVENTURE

Tristan Cotton

Marvin came out of the bathroom after brushing his teeth and headed to his room at 5:43 a.m. He was getting ready to go to the gym. He believed that the strength in all other areas of your life stemmed from the discipline of your body. He slipped on his sweatpants and gym shirt, grabbed a Gatorade from the fridge, and headed out. He unlocked the door to the gray Audi that was gifted to him for maintaining good grades all throughout high school.

When he arrived at the gym, he noticed the black Lexus parked a few spots down from him in the parking lot. Oddly enough, it had been there for days. It belonged to a popular body builder, Chaz "Da Body Man," who had millions of followers.

The first piece of equipment he used was the leg press machine.

Can't skip leg day, he thought to himself.

Several sets in, he then moved to the dumbbells. He worked with such intensity that he paid no attention to the bulging vein forming on his left forearm. He coasted through several more reps and sets before he noticed the light creeping in from the sky's horizon. He packed up and headed back home, sweaty and sore.

When he entered his home, his parents were still asleep. They didn't have to be up until he got ready to leave for school. He walked by their family portrait. He was an only child, and he resembled both of his African American parents, who were tall, brown-skinned, and into fitness. He headed upstairs to take a shower and checked the time again, which read exactly 7 a.m. After showering, he headed to his room. He wasn't too picky when it came to finding something to wear, but nobody wanted to look tired and lazy, so he located a dark-blue Polo shirt and blue jeans. He glanced in the mirror to straighten his shirt, aware of how clearly it revealed the perfectly outlined eight-pack that was sculpted earlier in the morning and how it complemented his six-foot frame. He kept his hair cropped low for easy maintenance.

He didn't have time to sit and eat, so he decided to stop by some place on his way to school, some eight miles away.

Cruising through the busyness of the Virginian streets, he stopped by a Dunkin' and bought a glazed donut and a small, iced coffee. He'd been told by a few people that he didn't seem like the coffee type, given his stature, but appearances can be deceiving. He paid and continued on his way to school.

As he approached the stop sign at the Wellington Road bus stop, he squinted his eyes at the girl a few feet ahead of him. He drove up and recognized her—Jennifer Gomez, a junior who he saw a lot at their high school. Marvin got her attention and eagerly, but calmly, offered her a ride to school, being that it would take a while for her to get there by foot. She smiled, agreed, hopped into the passenger seat, and they drove off.

Marvin usually had no problem with silence, but he didn't want to make her uncomfortable, so he asked her how her week was going. She was saying she was swamped with *work*. He was surprised but noted it was about another project she'd been working on. They eventually pulled into the student parking lot at school and hopped out of his car. Marvin was really looking forward to talking more about her project at lunch as they headed inside Arlington Community High.

Chapter 7

SERIOUSLY CURIOUS

Jonathan Taylor, Ralph Taylor III,
and Tristan Cotton

Marvin sat in the second row of his physics class. Mr. Thompson was almost done teaching about the theories of general relativity. Marvin knew that anything science-related wasn't really his strong suit, but something sparked his interest when Mr. Thompson was explaining it. He furrowed his eyebrows as Mr. Thompson went deeper into the mathematics behind the theory, speaking of how spacetime is a four-dimensional continuum that encompasses the three dimensions of space and one dimension of time, and how massive objects such as planets and stars "curve" this continuum, affecting the motion of nearby objects.

After a while, the monotony of Mr. Thompson's voice started to bore Marvin and his mind began to wander. He made a joke to himself about the bowtie Mr. Thompson was wearing and imagined it bending space and time around him. A smile crept onto his face. He reeled himself back in just in time for the bell to ring for lunch. He packed up his stuff and headed out.

As he's walking in the hallway, he couldn't help but think back to the lesson in physics. Science wasn't his forte, but he was amazed at the vastness of the universe, how complex it is, and the intricacies of its essence. He made his way inside the cafeteria through the swarms of freshmen, sophomores, and juniors.

People, Marvin thought to himself, a little annoyed. *There's so many of us.*

He made his way to the lunch line, which luckily wasn't that long.

Pizza. Sweet, he thought.

Arlington had pretty good school lunch compared to the other schools he'd attended.

As the line moved up, he felt a tap on his shoulder. He turned around and saw Jennifer, the girl he'd spoken to earlier that morning. He had almost forgotten they talked about meeting for lunch.

* * *

Jennifer started to drift off in her second period AP Calculus class. She already knew about what they were being taught, so she wasn't listening closely. Her mind drifted off to the mystery of the missing influencers. She had a thousand thoughts.

Why were they taken? Where were they put? Who's behind this? How would they even be found?

BEEP! Her thoughts were interrupted by the sound of the bell. Jennifer then quickly picked up her stuff and left. She was eager to talk with Marvin. Studying this case was hard. She felt as if she was missing something, so having someone else to talk to could help her figure out what she wasn't seeing.

She went down the black and white tiled steps past the red hallways covered in cheesy inspirational quotes and murals. When she entered the cafeteria, her eyes darted around, searching for Marvin in a sea of highschoolers. She saw him in the line, where they were serving her favorite school lunch—pizza. She ran up to join him.

After greeting Marvin, Jennifer asked, "Still want to talk?"

"Well, duh," he said jokingly. "I'm finally interested in this topic, and you already have a bunch of information on it. I want to see if I can add anything or help."

"That's awesome!" she said excitedly as they started walking towards a table. "I do have a lot of notes, but I am having trouble finding out where they all fit."

Once they sat down, Marvin immediately started eating his food while Jennifer took out her notes.

"Well, a good place we can start is who is being kidnapped," she said while straining to pull out her heavy notebook from her dense backpack. "So far there's been people taken or missing—people who speak on podcasts, some news anchors, singers, dancers, or even just plain rich people. BUT the thing they all have in common is that they are all influencers! If they have a pretty big following, then they have a chance of being taken."

"Well," Marvin said, swallowing his food, "why are they being taken?"

"That's the thing!" Jennifer said angrily, throwing her hands in the air. "Why are influencers just disappearing? Are they being kidnapped? Is it just a coincidence that they are all going away back-to-back? Where are they going?!"

"Calm down," Marvin said, gently reassuring her. "I have learned from my ROTC training that getting too emotional can slow down progress and make you think illogically."

Jennifer took a deep breath and thanked him. "You're right, it's just that people don't usually listen to me, and they think that I'm being irrational and paranoid," she said, holding her head down and rubbing a silver ring on her finger that she got from her friend a while ago for a birthday present.

"It's fine," Marvin said calmly. "I get it."

"Thanks, but anyways, the big thing that I have a problem with is the *why*. Why would they leave when they still have so much more to gain?"

They went on for the rest of lunch trying to figure out the *why* of this mystery. Frustratingly, neither of them could come up with a plausible answer. So, what they decided to do at the end of lunch was regroup at 6 p.m. at McDonald's so that they could talk more.

* * *

Jason got to school thinking about how he would apologize to Jennifer for leaving her on the road. Because of this, he couldn't focus very well in his other classes. He got destroyed while playing dodgeball in PE. His friend Jack noticed how distracted he was and asked him what was going on.

Jason was really scared to tell Jack because he wasn't sure if that would put either or both of them in danger, so he said, "Nothing."

"We've been friends since you moved here. You know you can trust me, right?" Jack said, trying to comfort him.

Jason told Jack what he had seen, but Jack thought it was out of character for Jason to talk about bands and kidnappings. He was sounding like the conspiracy theorists he hated so much.

"Uhh, you clearly haven't been getting rest. You should try and get some rest when you get home. And maybe you shouldn't eat Taco Bell before bed, it gives you nightmares."

What was this thing people kept saying about rest? He wasn't in bed dreaming; he was wide awake when he saw these things happen.

Jason shook his head and was sad that Jack didn't believe him, but he knew he sounded crazy. He continued to struggle to focus throughout the day while his friends— Jack, James, and John—kept trying to comfort him to no avail. They made the decision during lunch to try helping Jason by taking his mind off whatever was making him upset. But the constant thought of all the conspiracy theories being true kinda spoiled his appetite.

Jason wanted to grab a snack after school, but he steered away from Taco Bell. Instead, he went to McDonald's where he saw a familiar face.

This chance encounter would change the rest of his life.

Chapter 8

FOOD FOR THOUGHT

*Jonathan Taylor, Ralph Taylor III,
and Tristan Cotton*

Marvin was excited to meet up with Jennifer later on. Once he was sure she'd caught the bus to get home, he left the school. When he got home, he noticed neither of his parents' cars were in the driveway. He didn't think anything of it because they'd probably gone out. He headed upstairs to shower. It was about 3:45 p.m., so he had some time to chill. After his shower, he watched some TV. He ignored the uneasy feeling creeping into the back of his mind as he flipped through the channels.

"Another celebrity gone missing," the headline read. His interest was slightly more piqued than before as he listened in on the details surrounding the disappearance. He thought back to the conversation he had had with Jennifer earlier.

Marvin decided to watch the action flick *Training Day* starring none other than Denzel Washington. He could watch this movie for the rest of his life. He liked it because of the invaluable message it sends—you can live as if the ends justify the means, but in the end, justice will always prevail.

Afterwards, he set out to meet Jennifer at McDonald's. He pulled into the parking lot and headed on in. He scanned the place and spotted Jennifer talking to some tall, light-skinned dude. As he approached them, he knew he didn't recall seeing him before.

* * *

Before the meet-up at McDonald's, Jennfer arrived at home and decided to unwind and relax. Since her parents worked hard at their jobs, they weren't around for the majority of the day. They tried their best to make time for the family, but sometimes their jobs just took them away for a while. She had an older brother named Pierre that lived at home, but he got his first job a little while ago and they were putting him through the grinder. He was also a college student. Often times, he wasn't even around. Jennifer was happy that he was out and about and she had the house to herself. Tired from all of the stress that came with being an amateur detective, she decided to sleep until 5:10 p.m. and then get ready.

She woke up from her nap refreshed but starved. She had an enormous urge to eat something filling and unhealthy and was glad she was meeting up with Marvin. She was happy to see her brother was home. After asking him nicely for his keys, she hopped into his car that he had bought a while ago (her brother's job was about a half-hour walk and he didn't want to use up the gas money for it) and she drove off to the McDonald's. She arrived about ten minutes earlier than her and Marvin had planned.

Instead of waiting in the car, she decided to go in and get a small drink to help tide her over. She got to the register (after impatiently waiting in a pretty short line) and decided to get a mocha frappe instead. She then sat down, pulled out her phone, and played on it for a minute before looking up to see Jason walking toward the cashier. Anger started to wash over her, but she calmed down, knowing that it was pointless. She decided to ignore him and just relax.

Surprisingly though, she felt a hand touch her shoulder. She whipped her head around to see Jason standing next to her.

"Uh … hi," he said timidly.

"Really?" she said back to him while standing up.

"Well, I came over to say sorry for this morning," he said with his head down, making very little eye contact. "I know that I should have picked you up. I just had a bad night and … uh …"

"I get it," Jennifer sighed. "It's honestly fine. I also probably wouldn't have picked up a random …"

"Hey!"

A deep voice startled Jennifer and she let out a small scream as she turned around to see Marvin.

"Don't scare me like that!!" she yelled while letting out a chuckle.

"WOAH. My bad!" Marvin apologized, putting his hands up in the air and

stepping back. He had a deep voice like his dad. "You got the notes?" he asked.

"Notes for what?" Jason interrupted.

"And who are you?" Marvin asked as he looked Jason up and down.

Jennifer looked back and forth between them.

"Oh, well, Jason meet Marvin. Marvin meet Jason. Jason goes to our school."

"Hi, Jason," Marvin said giving him a fist bump.

Jason turned his attention back to Jennifer and said, "You still haven't answered my question. What notes?"

"Well," Jennifer said proudly, "I have been taking notes on this mystery that's been going on for a while. It's about people who have been going missing."

"Are you talking about the influencers?" Jason asked while his face went pale. He looked like he'd seen a ghost.

"Yeah," Marvin said, kind of concerned after noticing the change in Jason's facial expression.

"Have you heard about it? Do you have any idea what's going on?" Jennifer asked as she searched Jason's face for clues.

Jason looked down for a moment. He then looked up and stated, "I will tell you everything I know if you let me hang out with you guys."

Marvin shrugged his shoulders. "Works for me."

"Me too," Jennifer chimed in.

Jason sat down and his demeanor suddenly turned serious. His head swiveled as he made sure there were no threats nearby. Then, he lowered his voice and said, "I have seen things that no one else has seen, and I can help, but only if you let me in on what else is going on."

Marvin and Jennifer looked at each other and nodded.

"Yeah," Marvin said. "I'm down for it."

"And I absolutely agree!" Jennifer said. "We are going to need all the help we can get."

"Well," Jason said with a sigh of relief, "now that that's over, let's figure this mystery out."

Jennifer then pulled out a really thick binder and a black composition notebook. Jason's eyes widened. He was confused … and slightly concerned about her sanity.

"Why is it so big?!" he said loudly, causing everyone in the restaurant to look at him. Jason then slunk down into his seat, embarrassed by his loud outburst.

"It's really thick," Jennifer said quietly, "because I've been working on this for a long time. I have all the different influencers' data in here. Their hobbies, families, home locations, last time being seen, *everything*."

Jason looked at Marvin with even more concern and said, "Is she okay? Is this even legal?!"

"It's in the name of justice and serving the community … I guess," Marvin said with his head down, also embarrassed, but laughing quietly.

Jason looked at Marvin with an extremely straight face and said, "That's … stalking. What she is doing is stalking! Well, now that I think about it, discussing this at a small McDonald's like this is, kind of, I don't know, too open and awkward!" Jason said, looking around the room, noticing the faces of confusion and annoyance.

Jennifer looked at Jason and wondered if he was up for the job of figuring out this mystery. Marvin had the same thought and said, "Do you want to learn more about it or not?"

Jason responded flatly, "Yes, bro, that's why I'm here!"

Jennifer shook her head. "Okay, we're wasting time and ..."

"Oh man!" Marvin groaned. "I didn't even get to order!"

"No one said that you couldn't order," Jennifer said with a sigh. "Just order and then I have an idea. We will go to my house! Text your parents about being late and give them my address. You know how parents are! They want to know our every move."

She rolled her eyes to the sky as all of them agreed, nodding and verbalizing how parents are.

Marvin asked, "What is at your house again?"

Jennifer said, "I have multiple filled boards of information."

"How do you still have more information at home?" Jason asked, confused and now annoyed.

"Hey, I take this seriously, man," Jennifer said with a smirk. "With any hope, we'll get this done soon."

"I'll follow you," Marvin chimed in. "Jason, who are you riding with?"

Jason felt uncomfortable but he was indeed curious. He thought it best to ride with Marvin.

They ordered some food and all drove to Jennifer's house. Marvin parked his car at the curb.

"I have to talk to my brother first. He'll be weird about you two coming over and I want to make sure the coast is clear."

She told them to wait outside while she went inside. She entered the house and looked in the living room to find Pierre doing homework and vibing to a song by A'Shantie Bleu.

Pierre heard a creak from Jennifer's step and looked back. His face glowed from seeing her but he also looked a bit surprised.

"Pierre, you okay?"

He frowned a bit.

"I'm so tirrreeed," he said childishly. "These people don't know how to be patient at the register. They also are terrible at communicating."

Pierre worked early in the morning as a cashier at Walmart and people were more irritable at that time of day.

"I'm tired of dealing with adults acting like children. Like, grow up man!" he said, fed up.

"You should get a different job then if you hate this one so much," Jennifer said with an invisible "idiot" at the end.

"Trust me, I will as soon as I can find one," Pierre replied.

"Well, good luck with that," she said a little sarcastically.

"Speaking of good luck with a plan, how's that conspiracy theory coming along?" he asked with a laugh in his voice.

"It's more than a conspiracy. It is a big problem that is possibly a danger to us all!"

"It could be that or it could be that it's in your head and you're just being paranoid," he said with true sincerity in his voice, something Jennifer very rarely heard from him.

"I feel like this could be something bad, and I don't want anything bad to happen to us," she said with her face falling to the floor.

"I know, I know," Pierre said while also now looking down. "I get that you don't want to stop looking into this, but don't let it go too far. And if it's nothing, drop it."

"Thanks, man," she said, tearing up.

Even though Jennifer would not have admitted it, she was a little more at peace because of Pierre's speech. It was always a nice reminder that family still cared about her.

"Can we come in now?" Marvin asked as he popped part of his body inside the doorway.

Jennifer turned, stunned to see Marvin.

"Didn't I say wait outside!?" she said with her face scrunched up.

Pierre jumped up. "Who's him?" he asked, confused but now wanting to annoy Jennifer. "Is he your boy-"

Pierre was interrupted by a smack to the back of the head from his sister.

"No, he's not," she said, practically fuming. "He and Jason are here to help with my theory. We are classmates."

Jason slid in behind Marvin and waved sheepishly.

Pierre chuckled and while moving back to the couch he said, "Alright, no funny business y'all."

Jennifer rolled her eyes and signaled for Marvin and Jason to come in. They all went down the narrow staircase into the dark basement.

"Sorry, guys. The people who made the house put the light switch across the room," Jennifer said, shifting through the darkness to get to the switch.

As she turned on the bright lights, Marvin and Jason looked at the walls then back at each other to make sure they were seeing the same thing.

Covering the light-brown walls were photos, notes, and maps of all kinds that applied to the many influencers that had disappeared. There were also a few free-standing easels covered as well.

"Where'd you get the money for this!?" Jason asked as he roamed around the basement.

"Better question, how long have you been getting this information?" Marvin asked. He was the one concerned about her sanity now.

"Well, my mom and dad work a ridiculous amount of hours, so they provide me with the money I need for this," she said slightly flustered. "And I've been working on this for four years. They figured it was better than me hanging out in these streets, and they can easily keep an eye on me here."

"You've been working on this since you were thirteen!" Jason yelled in disbelief.

Jennifer's face flushed at Jason implying she was a bit unhinged.

"All right Jason, relax," Marvin said calmly, trying to look on the bright side. "We now have a lot, if not most, of the information we need. With all this at our disposal, we should be able to solve this in a snap!"

His words lifted Jennifer's spirit and gave her a little more pride in her work.

They all sat down. As Marvin started eating his food, they looked at the boards. They tried to find a pattern or something, but there were all kinds of people, from pastors to chefs to musicians to fashion designers and models. They did notice, after comparing them further, that they all had more than ten million followers.

"Wait, guys," Marvin said. "This person doesn't have ten million followers."

Jennifer and Jason walked over to see an influencer with 3.5 million followers, but his account was only six months old. He was rising and rising fast.

"Well, that means then," Jennifer said with a gasp, "that this abductor is not only stealing people who have a *zillion* followers but somehow they included this one person who has a lot of potential and is building their following in lightning speed."

After a while of looking without solid results, Jason frustratingly said, "There's no other pattern!"

"It's there," Jennnifer said. "We just have to look a little."

"We've been here for more than a half an hour and we've found *nothing!*" Jason yelled, flinging his hand in the air. It struck one of the easels, causing things to fall off the board.

"S-sorry" Jason said, kneeling down to pick up the stuff he'd knocked over.

"It's fine," Jennifer said. "We've just got to keep working. We'll find something eventually. We have to," she said very seriously but kindly.

Jason picked up the stuff to put it all back then noticed something. In one of the pictures of the singers, there was a van that was all too familiar. It was the same van that the company he worked for, Auditory Perception, used. The picture wasn't super clear, but it looked like their logo in the corner windshield.

"Wait, what? Guys, come see this!" Jason said, showing them the picture. "This is a car from the company I work for!"

"Huh?!" Jennifer exclaimed. "Why would your company car be in this picture?"

"The better question," Marvin asked, "is what business did they have in Pennsylvania when the company is in Virginia?"

Jason was shook. He didn't know what to say or think. Sure, he had been suspicious of some things, but there wasn't anything he could think of to make sense of this.

"Wait a minute!" Marvin said, running through his memories to find out what he remembered about this influencer. "Doesn't your company make those little dedication earbuds or whatever they're called?"

"Y-yeah," Jason said, nervous to find out what Marvin was about to say.

Marvin then went on his phone and pulled up the influencer on YouTube. He found one of her last videos.

"Guys, look," Marvin said, showing them his phone. "That influencer was promoting the earbuds from Jason's company!"

Jason's eyes widened while watching the video. Then he saw a man in the background that made the hairs on his arm stand up.

"It's … him," he muttered fearfully.

"Who's him? What's wrong?" Jennifer asked worriedly.

"His face … it's the man that took Adam Young. The band member. I saw it with my own eyes."

The color drained from Jason's face.

Jennifer stared at him intensely, desperate to know what he was talking about and hoping that he could give some information on the guy.

Marvin, however, was in shock about something else.

"Why didn't you call the police!?" he shouted.

"I wanted to but my boss told me not to tell anyone or else!" Jason said. "This is the information I told you I would share with you while we were in McDonald's. I, I just didn't want to believe it. It's actually a big reason why I wanted to talk with you guys—to see if that had anything to do with your conspiracy."

"Well, now you know," Marvin said, annoyed and frustrated.

Jason stammered, "You don't understand. He said he would take away my job and my family would be broke. Now that I'm thinking about it, it may have even been a threat."

Marvin nodded, not wanting to rattle Jason's nerves any more than they already were.

"I get it, Jason. I understand now. It's okay," Marvin said.

Meanwhile, Jennifer was on to something.

"It's the same," she whispered quietly.

"What?" Marvin asked.

"You guys, for about nine of the other influencers who went missing, they all were promoting those earbuds in one of their last videos," Jennifer said, now making a sticky note and putting it in the center of the room. "This means that these people are connected and the company you work for may have something to do with their disappearances, Jason."

Jason shut his eyes tight, wishing this was just a dream.

Marvin said, "So there are three common denominators. One: almost all of them have a lot of followers. As a matter of fact, they get the most views in their category, except for the one rising star. Two: they all have these earbuds. And three: they all promoted these same earbuds on their social media. I say we look for who else is promoting these air buds and see if they also have a lot of followers … or are rising stars. That should help us narrow down the next targets."

Jennifer smiled slightly, happy that they were making headway. Jason nodded in agreement, and they all started their search for who could be next, which was a longshot at best.

For the next hour, they worked on their phones, hitting as many categories as they could think of. At about 8 p.m., they reconvened to share their findings.

Chapter 9

CONNECTING THE DOTS

*Jonathan Taylor, Ralph Taylor III,
and Tristan Cotton*

They'd been searching meticulously, often revisiting the walls of clues that showed all the people who were already missing. Their data included social media information, number of followers, last known locations, posts, fans posts, and even posts by disgruntled stalkers. It was brutal. They looked at the maps where Jennifer had used pushpins to identify where the influencers were last seen.

Marvin gathered the group back together.

"Hey, let's see where we're at with our search," he said.

Jennifer said, "Let me go first. Jason saw Adam Young taken, and we believe that he is part of this whole conspiracy. He had around ten million followers and poof, he's gone! All of the ones on my board also had a massive amount of followers.

"Oh, boy. This is not sounding good," Jason mumbled.

"Okay, okay," Marvin said, feeling like they were getting somewhere. "How many of those were on the East Coast at the time of their last post or last sighting on social media?"

Jennifer went to her wall of clues and put pushpins in the locations. All of the influencers were on the East Coast when they went missing.

The three of them stood together staring at the wall of puzzle pieces slowly coming together.

"Who is left?" Jason asked.

Marvin and Jennifer looked at him at the same time.

Marvin asked, "What do you mean?"

"Well, who else fits this profile of having millions of followers and comes to the East Coast?"

Marvin and Jennifer attacked their phones, trying to narrow down who had millions of followers but was still active on social media. There weren't many of them left. As a matter of fact, only three people fit the criteria.

There was Roger Temple, a million-dollar real estate agent. This guy had over ten million followers on Twitter and Instagram and he sold high-end properties in New

York and the Hamptons. His social media showed he had broken his leg in a car accident, so they ruled him out.

Marissa Moreau was a sought-after interior designer in the U.S. and internationally, but her home was on the East Coast. She lived in Maine, which seemed too far away from D.C. based on the other kidnappings.

Then there was Christopher Steele, a bestselling author whose books had been turned into blockbuster movies. He had a massive home in Atlanta, but he was filming in Thailand.

There were plenty of rising stars, but they narrowed them down to three. They came to that conclusion because they looked at the trends of who was getting the most views over a short period of time. There were quite a few, but once they narrowed those down to the East Coast, only three possibilities met all of the criteria.

Jennifer said excitedly, "I can't believe we are doing this! We are cracking the code!"

Jason said, "Who are the three?"

"Well," Marvin began, "we have this guy Alonzo who remodels cars. In just two short weeks, he grew his fan base from one to five million. He lives in D.C. and he promoted those earbuds. Next, we have Grandma Betty. She's this senior lady who is also a comedian and her followers have grown a lot over the past month. She has won a lot of contests and is on tour with some of the top comedians in the world. She also has the earbuds, and she lives on the East Coast in Delaware. And finally, we have A'Shantie Bleu. She lives in Cali but is on the East Coast a lot. She also promoted the earbuds and ..."

Jason felt the world stop for a brief moment when he heard the name ... *A'Shantie Bleu ... A'Shantie ... Bleu ....* He thought back to a conversation that he had with his boss not so long ago over the phone. Mr. E. had asked him if he'd heard any of her music.

He snapped out of his thoughts, interrupting Marvin mid-sentence, and said rather gloomily, "She's next."

Marvin and Jennifer both looked at him and asked simultaneously, "How do you know?"

Jason shared his thoughts with them.

Jennifer looked her up and said, "She's originally from San Diego, but she is in D.C. right now, per one of her latest posts, at East Oasis Hotel."

Jason teasingly chimed in, "Stalking ..."

Jennifer replied, "Whatever. Pull her up on your phones."

While they were doing that, Jennifer started sending various pictures of A'Shantie to her printer so she could add them to the wall.

Jennifer and Marvin took a closer look at them once she posted them up. Jason focused on one picture of A'Shantie. It was undeniable how pretty she was, but he was captivated by the black truck that appeared in several of the pictures. He asked Jennifer if she had a magnifying glass. Using it to look closer, his eyes widened as he realized something. This time it was undeniable—the truck had the logo of the company he worked for.

Jason was visibly shaken.

"I think it's my boss that is doing this. That's why he was against me calling the police. I can't believe this," Jason said, saddened by this possible revelation.

"We have an obligation to protect the next victim," Jennifer stated like she was a police captain.

Jason shook his head like a bobble head. "No, no we don't! We don't even know for sure. It was just a hunch when I said she was next."

Jennifer had a light in her eyes as she smiled widely at the thought of what she was about to say. "Jason, it was a good hunch, and we are going to go with it. We are going to save A'Shantie Bleu!"

Chapter 10

INFLUENCER: A'SHANTIE BLEU

Essence Cotton

R&B singer and model A'Shantie Bloomfield lived in San Diego, California. She was twenty-four years old and had had a rough childhood. Her family was poor and didn't have much. A'Shantie was a good singer and often sang for her family when she was little. It was her lifelong dream to be a professional singer when she got older.

A'Shantie stood about 5'7" with brown skin, long curly hair, and hazel brown eyes. She was a mixed woman with African American and Hispanic heritage. Her mom was from Puerto Rico and her dad was from Los Angeles, California.

Although A'Shantie lived in San Diego, she flew to different places, like Baltimore, Maryland, because she had modeling gigs and friends in that area. A'Shantie's songs were about her life and how she grew up. She also sang about when she was poor and didn't have anything, and about how she often got bullied in school about her up-bringing.

As A'Shantie grew up and got bolder, she started to be more open and fearless. She often sang in contests and took first place.

One day, before she was discovered, A'Shantie needed money to buy some food for her family. She started singing on the street corner and people came over to watch, listen, and give her money. As they listened to her sing, they started recording her. One person posted a video on Facebook and it got lots of likes, comments, and recognition.

A'Shantie saw the video on Facebook because millions of people were reposting it. She returned the favor by commenting on the post, "Hey, that's me singing." People commented under her comment telling her that she was an amazing singer. Then they started following her and more people started recognizing her.

A'Shantie went viral and she started vlogging her activities. She would post about getting ready and how she got her day started. She showed people how she managed her life from sunup to sundown. She would often record herself getting ready to go model or sing for others. As she got older, she got into doing runway shows for aspiring designers. People came out to see her and screamed her name as she was modeling. It was during that time that she changed her last name to Bleu.

A'Shantie was growing more and more famous by the minute and more and more people were following her. Wherever she landed, lots of people recognized her and were posting her on social media. She was even interviewed on a few television news segments. Acting was next on her list.

Chapter 11

AN ILL-FATED TRIP

Essence Cotton

A'Shantie flew to Baltimore, Maryland, for one of her tour concerts where she was opening for a popular rapper. She was on social media scrolling when she started to notice that other famous singers weren't posting on their accounts as much or at all. She thought nothing bad of it and figured they were all taking a break, until it became evident that lots more famous influencers had disappeared from social media.

A'Shantie called her best friend, Niyah, and, as usual, she could barely get a word in before Niyah started with the compliments.

"Hey, A'Shantie. Gurrrlll, that lime green outfit with those neon six-inch heels was all that! You are trending everywhere. I gotta get me those shoes but in black."

"Uh, first you have to get a job," A'Shantie responded.

They laughed together and then Niyah said, "I have a job, thank you! You just don't like my dog-walking business."

"Yup, because you know I'm all kinds of allergic," A'Shantie agreed. "But look, have you noticed a lot of the top influencers just being ghost?"

Niyah paused. "Well, kind of. You know people be trying to find ways to stand out from the crowd. Maybe this is a publicity stunt."

"Hmmm, I don't think so. I'm suddenly not feeling safe," A'Shantie said, uneasily.

"Look, don't worry," Niyah told A'Shantie. "You are probably just overreacting. Listen, I have to go to my spa appointment. Hang in there. I'll call you later."

A'Shantie was suddenly drained and decided to take a nap. She fell into dream land and dreamt that her life was falling apart—her record deal fell through, her modeling job crashed, and she lost everything. She woke up in a cold sweat, panicking and scared. She then texted her manager to see if she was still signed to the record label and she was. She also called her modeling agent to see if she was still booked and she was. A'Shantie sighed, relieved and grateful.

After that dream, she thought it would be a good idea to hire some private security. She talked it over with her mom, who agreed. But her record company and modeling agency thought she was overreacting. When she was on a job, the venues were secured, but having her own private security was a different expense that they didn't want to pay for.

Forget that! A'Shantie thought. She'd been taking care of herself for years and this was no different.

She went out for a run—her favorite way to keep in shape and clear her mind. She had just received some new tiny yet powerful earbuds to try out from a popular brand. She loved them! As a matter of fact, she had agreed to do some social media promos for them. She found a good spot and went live before she hit the trail.

"Hey, everyone, it's your girl here, A'shantie Bleu. Let me tell you, I just got the Auditory Perception earbuds and they are fantastic! They have great noise canceling and the bass is unmatched. If you are looking for tiny earbuds with a lot of power, these are for you!" She made sure to tag the company as she looked at all of the likes and favorable comments on her post. Then, she went on her three-mile run.

When she got back to the hotel, there just happened to be flyers in the lobby for private security firms. She took down their numbers.

After a phone interview, A'Shantie decided to hire a guard named Mr. B. All of his references checked out and his fees were in her budget. She felt safe again.

A week later, A'Shantie was out with her friends in Washington, D.C. They'd decided to go to the museum and other touristy spots like *regular people*, but she did have her bodyguard. A'Shantie and her friends were having a good time and everything was going as planned … until it wasn't.

Chapter 12

FOLLOW THAT CAR!

Jonathan Taylor, Ralph Taylor III,
Tristan Cotton, and Essence Cotton

Once Jennifer made her announcement, there was no turning back. She found out that A'Shantie was going to be in D.C. with friends the next week on a Saturday because she had posted practically her whole itinerary on social media. It was a short trip from Arlington, Virginia, to D.C., so Jennifer enlisted Marvin's driving services. It was a crazy plan, but Marvin was excited to play detective while Jason was hesitant about the whole thing. Jennifer and Marvin spent considerable time convincing Jason to go with them.

Saturday finally arrived. Marvin suggested that they should all get walkie-talkies to communicate.

"I'm not getting out. I'll just stay in the car," Jason said adamantly.

Scratching his head, Marvin said, "Uh, it could be hours before we come back. Don't you want to see D.C.?"

With heat behind his eyes Jason shot back, "The only thing I want to see is home!"

Jennifer sighed. "Okay, stay here and let us know if you see anything suspicious. Who knows when we will catch the kidnapper in the act!"

Marvin and Jennifer rushed to follow A'Shantie, who had just recently left the relatively expensive East Oasis Hotel with friends, but they noticed she had a security guard.

Marvin massaged his chin and gently said, "I know you see she has protection. So, what are we doing here?"

Jennifer tossed her head back and sighed while looking at the sky to hide her disappointment.

She faced Marvin pleading, "Well, we're here now. Can you just humor me for a bit?"

He knew this meant a lot to her, so he agreed. Not only that, there was something oddly familiar about the guard, but the sleuths could not figure it out.

They followed A'Shantie's video diary and kept an eye on her. They also enjoyed D.C. and all the culture it had to offer. In the evening, Ashanti walked with her friends.

Jennifer and Marvin got really frustrated after following them for a while. They expected something to happen—a little sign of the criminal, maybe some suspicious activity, anything. But nothing of the sort happened.

Marvin pulled out his walkie-talkie and reported to Jason, "Alright, Jason, we are heading back to the car. We have nothing."

Jason, tired and frustrated, said, "This was the biggest waste of my day that I'm never getting back."

* * *

After A'Shantie and her friends left the museum, they went out to eat. Afterward, as they were walking back to their hotel room, A'Shantie was talking to her mom on the phone, telling her about her day and all that she had done. A'Shantie's friends were walking ahead of her to give her some privacy, and her bodyguard was behind her watching them.

Once A'Shantie got off the phone, she put in her new ear pods and began to play her music. All of a sudden, she heard a strange humming noise then felt unsteady, and almost fainted then fainted. But before she hit the ground, her bodyguard caught her.

A'Shantie's friends didn't know any of this stuff was happening behind them because they were too focused on their conversation. As she entered the black vehicle, A'Shantie was no longer in control of her thoughts.

* * *

Jennifer and Marvin could see A'Shantie on the phone, but they were slightly out of earshot so that they wouldn't be spotted easily. The commotion of cars was a nice cover for their assignment but it was unfortunate for A'Shantie, who was walking but stopped dead in her tracks. Her knees seemed to buckle, but before she hit the ground, her security guard caught her. She stood upright, then walked with the guard to the black vehicle that had the signature logo for Auditory Perception.

Jennifer exclaimed, "Oh my goodness! It's happening right before our eyes. We have to do something. Hurry, get back to the car!"

They ran together, Marvin afraid but Jennifer excited.

Marvin sprinted like a track star; he was an exceptionally fast runner and found out Jennifer was, well, *less* than exceptional when he hopped into his car, quickly strapped on his seatbelt, and started to pull off.

"Wait. Wait for me!" Jennifer yelled from outside of the car. Marvin came to an abrupt stop as she jumped in, out of breath, with a smirk on her face at almost having been left behind.

Jason, confused, asked, "What's going on you guys? Why were y'all running?"

At this point, Marvin was weaving in and out of traffic.

"They actually kidnapped her!" Marvin yelled in disbelief.

"What?!" Jason said incredulously.

As the van started to cross into the street the trio was on, Jason noticed that the man from the Owl City abduction was driving the car.

"It's hiimmmmm!" he confirmed with dread.

Both Marvin and Jennifer glanced at Jason like, "Had you been with us, we could have acted sooner."

Jason finally caught on to their current predicament and he was none too happy. "Wait a minute. Are we following them?" he asked

"We are in hot pursuit, so buckle up," Jennifer said with a grin while Jason hung his head.

* * *

A few hours later, A'Shantie woke up in a dark place trying to figure out what had happened and where she was. She began to hear footsteps approaching then the lights came on. She couldn't see who it was because her vision was blurry. By the time it came back, the person was gone but the light was still on. A few minutes later, the person came back into the room and A'Shantie realized that it was her very own bodyguard who she had hired for protection.

"Mis-ster B.? Why did you do this to me? Where am I?" she asked as she fought back the urge to burst into tears.

Mr. B. just looked at her with a blank stare, like he wasn't looking at her at all.

"Why? Why did you take me?!" she screamed, but he couldn't give her an answer. Robot-like, he turned away from her and she watched him go to the other side of the room and ascend a staircase.

She started yelling, "Let me out, let me out!" and banging on the bars with all her might.

A chorus of both male and female voices revealed, "You're stuck here with us! Yeah, we are all prisoners.

With her heart pounding, A'Shantie turned around slowly and saw all of the other people that were also locked up. She recognized a few of them and wondered how they got there. It was then that she noticed she had a roommate—Cierra, a chef.

In the cell next door to hers was Bruno, a musician. The cells were oddly connected but A'Shantie could see Alia, a dancer, and Chris, a rapper, through a small window. They could all communicate with each other by yelling.

Not many of the other people were awake yet, as if drugged, but A'Shantie asked the few who were awake what happened to them. Some began to explain how they got kidnapped. A'Shantie then told them what happened to her. They were all confused about why they were in a place that appeared to be a basement.

Cierra mused, "I wonder if we all have something in common?"

Everybody agreed and started chatting all at once until Bruno said, "Aren't we all famous influencers from the DMV area?"

Everybody agreed except A'Shantie. "Well, I'm from Cali, but I do a lot of work in the DMV. There is definitely a connection."

Alia folded her arms across her chest. "So, we're all famous influencers who live or work a lot in the DMV area. Other things we have in common are that all of us were somewhere with family or friends when this happened, and all of us blacked out, not knowing what happened afterwards."

A'Shantie said, "Yes, but does anyone remember hearing a strange humming noise in their ears?"

Cierra replied, "Wait, yes, that does sound familiar. I was wearing those earbuds, but they went missing after I got here."

A'Shantie nodded, "Me too. Anyone else have earbuds?"

A few of the influencers said yes, but now, no one had them.

"We need to figure out what's happening here," A'Shantie said, "and who these people are so we can plan how to get out of here. I know my mother is losing her mind looking for me. I feel sorry for them when she finds out!"

A'Shantie could really have used a run to clear her mind, but that was just a wish at this point.

Suddenly a fine mist filled the room. Before A'Shantie could ask, "What is that?" she found herself gagging then feeling groggy. She barely made it to her bed before she fell fast asleep.

Chapter 13

HERO ANTICS

Jonathan Taylor, Ralph Taylor III,
and Tristan Cotton

The trio followed the van for a long time. Marvin made sure to drive very slowly and far enough behind so that the driver wouldn't notice him. As they arrived at the edge of Arlington, Virginia, they entered a wooded area and soon came to the Blue Ridge Mountains. In that area was a giant compound that the van was headed toward. Jason observed that it was the same area Ambrose had purchased from his family, and he mentioned that to Marvin and Jennifer.

Those two knew that they couldn't just go in there and tell Ambrose to release the captives. They didn't know Ambrose at all, nor did they know what he looked or sounded like. So they decided to get Jason to go in. He seemed to be on board. Well, not exactly.

"Are you insane?!" Jason asked.

Jennifer responded, "You're the only one who this guy knows, and he trusts you … at least a bit more than us strangers."

Marvin then chimed in, "Also, you going up there is the least suspicious thing out of the three of us. Employees go up to their bosses all the time."

"At their house?!" Jason asked as he blinked and cocked his head to the side.

After some more arguing and groaning, Jennifer and Marvin just barely convinced Jason to go along with the plan. Marvin insisted that Jason drive the rest of the way while he decided to hunker down on the floor behind the front seat, where he barely fit. Jennifer agreed to go into the awfully large trunk.

Jason wasn't very experienced behind the wheel. The constant swaying and bouncing of the car was evidence to Marvin that Jason wasn't doing too good of a job avoiding any bumps on the road.

"Careful with my car! My parents just bought it for me, and as you see, it's beautiful. Don't put a scratch on it!" Marvin yelled from the floor behind the front seat.

"Oh, wow, an Audi. I see you have wonderful taste in cars," Jason said sarcastically.

"Fool, I will get up and beat you up until your favorite colors are black and blue," Marvin shot back.

"I don't even want to be here or driving for that matter!" Jason yelled.

"I don't care. Don't scratch my car!" Marvin fired back.

In response to Marvin, Jason sped up then slammed on the brakes.

"Alright, alright!" Jennifer yelled from the trunk. "Let's focus. Jason, you need to get inside and stall Ambrose while Marvin and I try to find a way in, find the influencers, and get them out."

"Whatever," Jason responded, as he drove timidly to the gated entrance.

There was a camera and intercom on the driver's side, connected to the security inside to watch people outside. Jason nervously drove to the camera, start-stopping the brakes until he got as close to the intercom as possible, while Marvin seethed on the floor about Jason's jerky driving.

Jason rolled down his window, and immediately a security guard came online and said, "Who are you and why are you here?"

Jason tried to conceal his nervousness and said, "I'm here to see my boss, Ambrose."

"Why?" the guard asked sternly. "I don't see you as having an appointment."

Jason gulped and said, "I need to see the boss. It's quite urgent and kind of private."

The guard went silent for a moment. Jason was anxiously waiting. He couldn't help but be worried about all the bad things that could possibly happen to him and the amount of trouble he and his family could get into. Looking back, he still didn't know how he got into *this* situation.

With a beep and green light, the massive iron gate swung open. Jason proceeded to drive in with caution. He was doing his best to stay calm. As he approached the front door, he could only go so far. The driveway was circular and within the circle was a large tree statue that also served as a water fountain. He stopped the vehicle about twenty feet from the massive front door.

"Look," Jason explained, "I'm going to go and see if he'll let me in. I guess you two will be out here looking around. But after ten minutes if we don't find anything, promise me we'll leave. If you can't promise me that, I'm not going in."

Marvin, who was cramping up from being squished on the floor, agreed and Jennier balked, "Ten minutes? This place is huge. Can we make it twenty?"

Jason turned crimson and said between gritted teeth, "Ten minutes!"

Before any more could be said, he undid his seatbelt and opened the car door.

Marvin encouraged him. "You got this Jason."

"Yeah, yeah," Jason mumbled as he exited the car, unsure of what he was doing.

His stomach was flip-flopping and his nerves were on edge. He was worried about everything that could possibly go wrong, especially what would happen if they got caught. But he gathered up all of the courage he had left and approached the front door.

Chapter 14

IT'S NOW OR NEVER

*Jonathan Taylor, Ralph Taylor III,
and Tristan Cotton*

Not seeing a doorbell, Jason started to use the heavy knocker. But his boss, Ambrose, swung open the door, his figure casting a shadow in the large doorway.

"Jason?" Ambrose asked warily.

"Hello, Sir," Jason responded awkwardly, his voice cracking on the last word.

"What are you doing and how did you get here? You can't drive," the scientist said as he began to sweat a bit.

Who drove him here? Does this mean he brought his parents or the police? Ambrose wondered. He had no answers, but he knew Jason did not arrive by accident. He had a purpose for being there, and there weren't many good ones coming to Ambrose's mind.

"I can drive, just not legally," the young student replied in a tone of voice that gave off a "what am I saying!?" vibe.

Ambrose picked up on this and gave Jason an incredulous look. The boy was very clearly hiding something.

"Let me get this straight," Ambrose said stroking his chin. "You illegally drove to the Blue Ridge Mountains, to *my house*, by yourself?" The older man said in an accusing tone.

Now Jason started to sweat.

He fought to not start hyperventilating as he responded, "I, I wanted to see what became of the land you bought, and I see you spared no expense in making yourself a mansion." Jason looked around as if admiring his surroundings. "Looks like, uh, I should get a raise … yeah, get a raise … and that's why I'm here!" Jason said as he bit his lower lip, wanting to get out of there as soon as possible. He was just not a good liar.

Ambrose furrowed his brow and started shaking his head.

"Let's get out of this doorway and sort this out," Ambrose said as he ushered Jason inside.

Jason hesitantly entered, hoping he would be able to exit the home as easily as he got in. He glanced at his watch. There were six minutes left. He stood in the massive foyer. Floors of marble and a large statue of justice with the scales greeted him at the entry way. How ironic! There was so much to see and it was hard to put it all into words, but he was quickly thrust back into why he was really there.

Ambrose clasped his hands behind his back and started pacing the floor.

"As I recall, I helped your family and even jump started your dream career. You know what I think? I think you are lying. And I must say given your character, I'm afraid to know why you would feel the need to do so, unless … you know something?" Ambrose raised an eyebrow.

Jason swallowed hard as if digesting a golf ball.

Based on Jason's reaction, Ambrose knew he had hit the nail on the head. But just then, a soft yelp caught the businessman's attention, and his eyes darted toward the direction of the sound.

He asked Jason, "Did you hear that?"

Not at all, Sir!" Jason said loudly, trying to direct Ambrose's attention away from the noise he knew to be his friends.

Ambrose sighed. He already knew by Jason's actions that there were others on the grounds. Of all the days to give his additional security the day off.

Let's deal with one problem at a time, Ambrose thought.

Ambrose made a hand gesture to Bastian. The message was clear: *comb the grounds and bring the trespassers to me.*

Jason knew what was happening but there was nothing he could do to stop it.

Bastian went into his security office where there were multiple cameras covering every square inch of the mansion. Bingo! He found them on camera four, checking a window on the left side of the mansion for a way inside. He and Bastian snuck outside and caught them off guard as they were peering into windows.

"You two, halt! You are trespassing on private property. I need you to come inside right now!" Bastian yelled.

Marvin and Jennifer froze as they turned slowly to face the same guard who had taken A'Shantie. Getting caught was not a part of their plan.

Marvin, moving protectively in front of Jennifer said, "No, you can't make us come inside. Matter of fact, we're leaving and we're going to take Jason with us."

Bastian smiled as he revealed a stun gun. "Either you are coming willingly or by force. What's it going to be?" he asked.

Bastian walked them into the estate and soon all three friends were together again in the foyer, but it was not a happy reunion. Jason noticed Jennifer had a limp. She had not seen a sprinkler in the grass and twisted her ankle on it, which was the noise Ambrose heard.

Jason shook his head, eyeing Marvin and Jennifer with angry eyes, as if saying, *This was the dumbest plan ever!*

Ambrose grimaced at the three students who had made their way to his home. He was actually in disbelief but impressed at the same time. Clearly, they knew something.

This, Ambrose thought to himself, *is not ideal.*

He asked, "So why are you three here? And since you are trespassing, you can be arrested as prowlers. I'm thinking of doing just that!"

Jennifer was shaken, but she refused to be bullied. Her voice was shaky, yet firm. "We know what you've done, Mister. Where are those influencers?"

Ambrose's eyes bucked. "Little girl, you don't know what you are saying."

Jennifer's eyes became little slits. "You know *exactly* why we're here. If you have nothing to hide, let us search the house!"

Jason was shaking his head in deep protest, but as usual, they were not paying attention to him.

Ambrose was abrupt but also clearly irritated. "You've got some nerve asking to search my home. Take them to the basement, Bastian. Let them start down there." Ambrose, however, had a different idea.

"I'm not going!" Jason yelled as he tried to back up to the front door. Nothing good ever happens in the basement."

But Bastian showed his taser, and Jason knew he was not able to escape.

Ambrose's tone was authoritative. "MOVE."

Bastian ushered them down a long hallway to a doorway that led to the lower level. Jennifer needed to use the railings to support her aching ankle. Marvin helped where he could.

The basement was huge. Table tennis, video games, a home theater, and a pool table were all strategically placed. There was a popcorn machine and a beverage vending machine. It looked like a cool place to hang out, but under different circumstances.

Soon they came upon the newest basement renovation of connected rooms, and that's when the trio saw several of the missing influencers. A few of them looked as if they had just awoken from a deep sleep. Some were even asking for help.

Marvin and Jason were stunned by their current reality, but they were also alarmed at seeing the influencers imprisoned and wondered about their fate. Marvin was rendered speechless when he saw the fitness instructor whose car had been parked at the gym for days.

Jennifer exclaimed, "I knew it! I knew you did it. What kind of person are you? You should be ashamed of yourself."

Ambrose peered down at Jennifer. "What kind of person am I? Why, I'm a genius! All I wanted was to put a small implant into these influencers so I wouldn't have to worry about my control over them failing due to their earbuds dying. Yes, my earbuds have, shall we say, special powers. They infiltrate a person's soul. Then they would only promote my products so my tech company would continue to grow bigger and bigger. That way, my company wouldn't have to rely on the whims of society and what they liked or disliked at any given time. Even when I created my business and got away from all the ingrates who wanted nothing to do with my genius technology just because I look *different,* my company was at the mercy of trends and popularity."

Ambrose was aware he was explaining his entire plan, but he had a plan to keep them quiet, so he allowed himself to monologue.

"I refuse to have *this* much money, *this* much success, and *this* much fame for my brand and *still* have to answer in some way, shape, or form to someone who flips bottles or plays video games and happens to be *funny!* The fact that any of these people are at half my level of wealth is an insult to all true worth and intelligence, and one I will not let slide. The will of the people is faulty if they spend their lives gawking at some person who documents and publishes their life for others' viewing pleasure."

Taking a deep breath once his tirade was over, Ambrose got a drink from his vending machine and contemplated his next move. But his contemplation was cut short by the sound of sirens outside.

Bastian looked confused. "Boss, did you call the police?" he asked as he peered at his phone and saw that the mansion was surrounded by multiple police cars.

Ambrose was incensed. "No ... I ... did ... not!" he said through gritted teeth. "Wait! Did one of you do this?!?" he hissed at the teenage group.

The friends looked at each other, then Jason said with a smirk, "It was me! I did it before I reached your front door. I used voice command to call them, but honestly, I wasn't a hundred percent sure it worked. And guess what? I've also had my phone on record the entire time," Jason said as he pulled the phone out of his pocket, showing he was telling the truth.

"Now that's what's up!" Jennifer commended as the three friends hugged in victory.

Cheers from the kidnapped influencers filled the room, and Ambrose sank to his knees in defeat, knowing there was nothing he could do but hire a lawyer and wait for his fate to be determined.

Chapter 15

EPILOGUE: JUSTICE PREVAILS

Catherine Taylor

Facing twelve federal kidnapping charges, along with a host of other charges, Mr. Ambrose White was unsurprised when he was sentenced to life in prison. Since he could no longer attend board meetings, he needed to appoint an employee who could handle the daily operations of his business. At least that *was* the plan.

But there was a problem. Normally, when a business owner goes to jail, the business does not cease to operate. But while Ambrose tried to keep the number of people in on his scheme small, enough people knew and were charged, so his business could no longer run. When he and his subordinates fell, his company fell with them. Even if Auditory Perception could run, no one would ever trust his brand again.

Ambrose realized that for all the money, fame, and power he had, he was alone and no closer to being as powerful or coveted as he wanted to be when he first started his quest.

What good was all that he had achieved if he had not really helped anyone? If he had no one to share it with? What good was his money with no reason to use it? It would waste away with him. And then when he was gone, he'd have no idea what happened to it. It was in prison, with hours to contemplate his actions, that he finally began to understand the value of free will.

Ambrose's cellmate, Daryl, an old gruff fellow with white hair and a weathered face, shared with Ambrose things he had come to recognize in prison. Daryl's insights were even more valuable to Ambrose than the newfound time on his hands.

One day, half a year into his life sentence, Ambrose found himself explaining what had landed him in jail.

Daryl could see that the point of free will was lost on Ambrose, so he explained, "Many people misuse their free will more often than not. But love isn't love if it is not freely given, just as goodwill isn't goodwill if it isn't your will. You wanted what many people want: money, control, fame, and power, all meaningless if the point is only to satisfy yourself. Even worse, you thought that it mattered so much that you got what you wanted that you made other people's will conform to yours," the old man said sagely with sadness and regret in his eyes.

"But now you're realizing that being covetous has only made you greedy and lonely, and you wasted quite a long time trying to fill that void with material things. But you don't have to waste your life. Happiness that lasts doesn't come from being self-centered, but by putting others first," Daryl finished, sure his words were getting through to Ambrose.

The younger man reflected on this awhile, and the next morning resolved to not waste another day of his life. He began seeing how he could help others be productive citizens upon their release by teaching technology classes.

Bastian was not implicated as part of a plea deal, and he was free. He was a pawn in a wicked game of chess, used and controlled by Ambrose. Ambrose had stacks of cash in various places in his home. Through his attorney, he ensured Bastian and his sister were well cared for, possibly for the rest of their lives.

All of the influencers survived the ordeal, although a few of them greatly reduced their social media presence all-together. They decided it wasn't worth it, as they could attract some other crazed fan who wanted to cause them harm. Others capitalized on the experience by going on talk shows and news segments, writing books, and doing personal appearances. A'Shantie Bleu's career took off, as fans rallied to support her. Her management team finally provided her with top-notch security.

Although Jason was a critical part of Ambrose's demise, Ambrose ensured he and his family were secure. Several tech companies clamored for Jason's attention, so he was in good shape.

As for the three friends, well … there were rewards for the whereabouts of a few of the influencers, so they shared the pot of money. Jennifer knew she wanted to start her own detective agency after college. People were already asking her to find things like lost pets, and she took every case *seriously*. Marvin helped out too, and Jason was never far behind. They were all over social media and the news thanks to their heroics.

Suddenly, they were influencers!

ABOUT THE AUTHORS

Essence Cotton

Essence Cotton is a seventeen-year-old high school senior. She likes to have fun and talk with her friends. She enjoys listening to music in her room and loves watching TV shows from her childhood.

Tristan Cotton

Tristan Cotton is a seventeen-year-old high school senior attending a Baltimore County high school. He enjoys reading, excels in mathematics, and has an eye for the arts.

Catherine Taylor

Catherine Taylor is a seventeen-year-old, eleventh-grade honor roll student enrolled in the Building and Construction Magnet Program at her high school. She is a born leader with a creative mind and a passion for serving the Lord with excellence in everything she does.

Jonathan Taylor

Jonathan Taylor is a fourteen-year-old, ninth-grade honor roll student. Jonathan plays percussion instruments for his high school's concert band. He is an extremely creative and thoughtful young man who is always looking for ways to make life easier and better for others.

Ralph Taylor III

Ralph Taylor III is a fifteen-year-old, tenth-grade honor roll student. Ralph plays the trumpet in his high school's marching band. He is a charismatic young man with a servant's heart and cool hair.

William Taylor

William Taylor is a twelve-year-old, seventh-grade honor roll student. He plays saxophone for his school's band, sings in the school choir, and plays on the school's tennis team. He is an exciting and energetic young man who enjoys being athletic and participating in outdoor social activities.

publish your gift

CREATING DISTINCTIVE BOOKS
FOR LEADERS AT THE TOP OF THEIR FIELD

We're a collaborative group of creative masterminds
with a mission to empower leaders to share their unique
knowledge, insights, and experiences with the world.

Our expertise bridges the gap between
their wisdom and ideal readers—delivering impactful
self-help books that inspire lasting growth and change.

Want to know more?
Write to us at info@publishyourgift.com
or call (888) 949-6228

Discover great books, authors, and more at
www.PublishYourGift.com

Connect with us on social media

@publishyourgift

www.ingramcontent.com/pod-product-compliance
Lightning Source LLC
Chambersburg PA
CBHW060556100726
47907CB00005B/1384